DATE DUE

W9-CUT-853

JFic   Komaiko, Leah.
Kom   Annie Bananie---best
         friends to the end

PROSPECT SIERRA SCHOOL LIBRARY
2060 TAPSCOTT AVENUE
EL CERRITO, CA 94530
(510) 232-4123

PROSPECT-SIERRA SCHOOL LIBRARY

DEMCO

Annie Bananie
Best Friends to the End

Leah Komaiko

illustrated by
Abby Carter

Delacorte Press

Published by
Delacorte Press
Bantam Doubleday Dell Publishing Group, Inc.
1540 Broadway
New York, New York 10036

Text copyright © 1997 by Leah Komaiko
Illustrations copyright © 1997 by Abby Carter

All rights reserved. No part of this book may be reproduced or transmitted in any form or by any means, electronic or mechanical, including photocopying, recording, or by any information storage and retrieval system, without the written permission of the Publisher, except where permitted by law.

The trademark Delacorte Press® is registered in the U.S. Patent and Trademark Office and in other countries.

Library of Congress Cataloging-in-Publication Data

Komaiko, Leah.
    Annie Bananie—best friends to the end / Leah Komaiko.
        p.   cm.
    Summary: Libby plans to give Annie Bananie a spectacular Lucky Lunch Day in hopes of securing her as a best friend.
    ISBN 0-385-32112-0
    [1. Friendship—Fiction.]   I. Title.
PZ7.K8347Ah   1997
[Fic]—dc20   96-24341
                                        CIP
                                        AC

The text of this book is set in 17-point Perpetua.
Manufactured in the United States of America
May 1997
BVG   10   9   8   7   6   5   4   3   2   1

To: Jenny, the Dawes Gang,
my Putchies, and
Mrs. Liebling, wherever you are

Annie Bananie
Best Friends to the End

Chapter

1

"Hey, new girl!" yelled Eddie Armstrong. "You with the curly red hair!"

It was Annie Bananie's first day at Nichols School. She looked over at Eddie.

"Yes, you!" Eddie laughed. "No dogs allowed."

"The dog's name is Boris, Eddie," said Libby Johnson. Libby stood on line outside the school next to Annie Bananie. Annie's dog, Boris, sat right by Annie's side.

"Is the new girl blind, Libby?" Cindy

Simon asked. Cindy was the smartest girl in the class.

"No, I'm not blind," Annie Bananie said. Then she stared at Cindy so that Cindy could get a good look.

"Oh," Cindy said. "Because if you were blind, Boris could be your Seeing Eye dog. Seeing Eye dogs are permitted in schools and other public places," she added.

"If the new girl's not blind, why does she have a dog here?" Eddie asked.

"For your information," Libby said louder so that everyone could hear, "the new girl is my friend Annie Bananie."

What Libby really wanted to say was that Annie Bananie was her new best friend. But she knew three other girls in the class would want to say the same thing. The girls had met Annie Bananie over summer vacation. But Libby had met Annie Bananie first.

"Hi, you guys!" Annie said. Her voice was big and friendly. Annie shook her hair so that Eddie could see how curly and red it was. "This is my best friend, Boris. He likes to go everywhere I go."

Boris barked. His bark was huge, and so was he.

"Whoa, Big Boris," Eddie said. "You could eat my dog for lunch!"

"What kind of a name is Annie Bananie?" Cindy asked.

"What kind of a dog is Boris?" Michael Chang wanted to know. Michael was afraid of dogs.

"He's a flesh-eating monster," Eddie said.

"No he's not." Annie laughed. "Boris is a vegetarian."

"So, what's a vegetarian?" Michael asked.

"That means he doesn't eat meat," Cindy said.

"Boris is a rottweiler," Libby said. "That's a purebred dog."

"Meowwww." Bonnie Baker butted into the line between Annie Bananie and Libby.

"Meooow! Move, Libby!" Bonnie said. Then she smiled so that everyone could see how big and white her teeth were.

Bonnie was the prettiest girl in the class. More than anything, Bonnie wanted to be a cat. Next she wanted to be Annie Bananie's best friend. She was one of the three girls who had met Annie over the summer.

"Look, Bonnie," Eddie said. Then he pointed at Boris. "There's a dog!"

"Duh and a half," Bonnie said. "Besides, me and Boris are already best friends. Even if I am a feline. Right, Boris?"

Bonnie scratched Boris under his chin.

She smiled at Annie Bananie. Annie Bananie smiled at Bonnie.

"So, Annie Bananie," Bonnie said, "ready for a tour of Nichols School?"

"I can show her," Libby said. "I got here first."

"Who cares?" Bonnie meowed.

Libby looked at Annie. Suddenly Annie looked like she was going to be sick.

"I have to go home!" Annie said. "I forgot to bring Boris his lunch!"

"Boris can have part of my lunch, Annie," Debbie offered.

Debbie was the second girl who had met Annie before school started. Debbie also wanted Annie Bananie as her best friend. Mostly Debbie liked to read books or grunt like a pig.

Debbie looked inside her lunch bag. "Oink. No meat!" She handed the bag to Annie.

"Thanks, Debbie," Annie said in her happiest voice.

"It'll be good." Debbie smiled.

Libby knew Debbie was right. Debbie always had good lunches. Libby didn't want to look inside her lunch bag. Whatever her mother had put in there, Libby knew it wouldn't be good enough for Boris.

Bonnie peeked into her lunch box. Eddie tried to look inside it, too.

"Hisssss." Bonnie snapped her lunch box shut. "Get your own lunch for once, Snowman. We call him Snowman because he's got so much dandruff," Bonnie said to Annie Bananie.

"Yeah, right, Bonnie," Eddie said without looking up. Then he scratched his head.

"The Snowman picks his dandruff all day long." Bonnie laughed. "He likes to watch it fall out of his hair. Then he eats it."

"I'll get you, Bonnie," Eddie said. He ran after Bonnie.

"Meoowwww, right." Bonnie laughed. "Snowman's lunch is a dandruff sandwich. And a delicious dandruff dessert."

Bonnie ran faster.

Annie shook her head. She scratched her hair with all her might. Then she looked on her shoulders to see if any snow had fallen.

Riiiinnng!

Everyone had forgotten over vacation how loud that bell was.

"Straight line, everybody," Cindy called out.

The line started to move. Libby felt excited.

"You'll like Mrs. Liebling," Libby said

to Annie Bananie. "She's the very, very best teacher."

"Walk in front of Boris so the teacher can't see him, will you, Libby?" Annie asked.

"Okay," Libby said.

"Now whatever you do, Boris," Annie said, "you behave. I don't need to get into trouble my first day of school!"

"Me neither," Libby grumbled under her breath.

Chapter

2

The second Boris's paw touched the school floor, he ran.

"Heel, Boris!" Annie called.

But Boris was too excited to stop. He pulled Annie Bananie and Libby all the way down the hall to Mrs. Liebling's room.

"Dog!" Michael jumped up on his seat.

"Well, I'll be dog-darned," Mrs. Liebling said.

"Call 9-1-1," Bonnie meowed.

"That's enough," Mrs. Liebling said. "Sit!"

Everyone sat. So did Boris. The only people standing were Annie Bananie and Libby. Mrs. Liebling looked Boris right in the eye.

"You must be my new girl," Mrs. Liebling said.

Everyone laughed.

"I'm the new girl," Annie Bananie said.

"Well, welcome, Ann Beth," Mrs. Liebling said.

"That's not Ann Beth," everyone said. "She's Annie Bananie."

"Ann Beth was my old real name," Annie Bananie said. She pointed to Mrs. Liebling's list. "But I'm Annie Bananie now. I changed my name officially."

"Oh, I see." Mrs. Liebling smiled.

Everybody looked at Annie Bananie. Nobody knew anyone who had changed their name officially.

"And who is this?" Mrs. Liebling asked. She scratched Boris's chin.

"Boris!" the whole class called out.

"I told Boris he probably couldn't come to school," Annie explained. "But he's a baby. He was afraid to stay home alone."

"Can we call your mother to pick Boris up?" Mrs. Liebling asked.

"My mom works," Annie said. She pulled the chain around her neck so that Mrs. Liebling could see her key.

"Gotcha, pardner," Mrs. Liebling said.

Mrs. Liebling was dressed like a cowgirl. She had on a denim dress, red leather cowboy boots, and a bandanna around her big ponytail.

Mrs. Liebling closed the classroom door. "It can be a little frightening when you're the only new kid on the prairie, can't it?" she asked. "Boris can stay. But only today and only until we can get your baby-sitter or somebody to pick him up.''

"Yes!" everyone shouted. Michael closed his eyes.

"Meowww." Bonnie pouted. "Can I bring my cat tomorrow?"

"Nope," Mrs. Liebling said.

"But how come Annie Bananie is the first person ever who gets to have a pet?" Bonnie whined.

"She got lucky," Mrs. Liebling said. "Boris is the first and last four-legged visitor in history. This is a school for children. Not animals!"

Just then the classroom door swung open and a girl galloped in.

"That's just Nina," Cindy said to Annie Bananie.

"She's been like that since kindergarten," Eddie said. "She's mental."

Nina galloped fast to the back of the room and shook her head from side to side. She made a noise with her lips like the horse was tired and needed a drink of water. Everybody laughed. Annie couldn't take her eyes off Nina. Boris tugged on his leash. Then he lay down and watched Nina with one eye.

"Howdy, Nina," Mrs. Liebling said. "I'm so happy to see you again. Say hello to our new friend. This is Annie Bananie."

"Neigh, Annie Bananie." Nina smiled. "We met this summer," she said to Mrs. Liebling.

"Neigh, yes!" Annie Bananie said. "Neigh."

Everyone looked at Annie Bananie. Nobody had ever neighed in public with Nina before.

Nina trotted in a circle around her desk.

Mrs. Liebling reached into her desk drawer.

"I brought something back from the ranch," she said. Mrs. Liebling had grown up on a ranch in Montana. Every summer vacation she went back to visit. Every fall she brought back a souvenir.

"Who can tell me what this is?" Mrs. Liebling asked. She took a big, tall cowboy hat out of a bag.

"I believe that's a special sheriff's hat," Cindy said.

"Not quite, Cindy," Mrs. Liebling said.

Annie Bananie raised her hand. "That's a ten-gallon hat! Right, Boris?" Boris opened both eyes.

"That's right, Annie Bananie," Mrs. Liebling said. "And just how does Boris know about a ten-gallon hat?"

"My uncle Dan has one," Annie said. "He has a ranch in Utah. Boris and I go there every summer."

"You're a lucky girl, Annie Bananie," Mrs. Liebling said.

Everybody just looked at Annie Bananie.

"Yes, but we couldn't go this summer," Annie said, "because we moved. But we'll go next summer."

"I can go with you." Bonnie meowed.

"Summer is a whole year away," Eddie groaned. "No holidays."

"Oh, really?" Mrs. Liebling asked. "Have you forgotten about Lucky Lunch Day? We have that next Monday in honor of the start of the new school year. Remember?"

"Oh yeah," Debbie said.

"That's the one day when we don't have to eat our own lunches or get poisoned in the cafeteria," Eddie said.

"Who will tell our new friend Annie

Bananie what Lucky Lunch Day is?" Mrs. Liebling asked.

Sifredo raised his hand. He winked at Annie Bananie. Sifredo always winked at girls. "On Lucky Lunch Day we each go to somebody's house for lunch instead of eating here at school," Sifredo said. "Those kids whose moms work at jobs go to a kid's house where the mom doesn't work."

"My mom doesn't have a job now," Bonnie meowed. "So Annie Bananie can come to my house."

"My mom doesn't work, either," Libby said.

"Yeah, but your mom just had a baby," Bonnie said.

"Congratulations, Libby!" Mrs. Liebling said. "Is it a boy or a girl?"

"A baby brother," Libby said. "His name is Daniel. But I can still have Lucky Lunch Day."

"For Lucky Lunch Day," Cindy said, "we pick names from a basket to see who goes with who." Then she smiled at Annie Bananie.

"Very good, Cindy," Mrs. Liebling said. "And remember, the most important thing about the day is friendship. It doesn't matter whom you have Lucky Lunch Day with. When you have a friend, everyone is lucky."

Libby looked at Annie Bananie.

"I'm going to be the luckiest," Libby grumbled under her breath.

Chapter

3

"So can you sign my permission slip for Lucky Lunch Day?" Libby asked her mother. Libby was setting the table for dinner.

"I don't see why not, Cookie Pie," Mrs. Johnson said.

"But can we have something good?" Libby asked. "And it has to be vegetarian."

"And why's that?" Mrs. Johnson asked.

"Because Annie Bananie doesn't eat meat."

"Oh, really!" Mrs. Johnson smiled.

"And how do you know you'll get Annie Bananie for Lucky Lunch Day?"

"Because I've never had Annie for lunch or a sleepover since she moved here," Libby said. "Besides, it's my turn to be lucky. I can feel it in my bones."

Grandma Gert came into the kitchen. Grandma Gert lived with the Johnsons.

"Aggh," Grandma Gert said. "If I don't eat soon there's going to be nothing left of me but skin and bones."

The baby screamed.

"Annie Bananie doesn't have to listen to a baby scream all day," Libby grumbled.

Grandma Gert was partly deaf. Right now Grandma Gert couldn't hear the baby screaming, but she did hear Libby.

"Aggh," Grandma Gert said. "Don't grumble. It's bad manners." Then she stuck her fingers into a pot of mashed potatoes sitting on the stove.

"Cookie Pie, will you please call your father and Carl for dinner?" Mrs. Johnson asked.

"Dinner!" Libby yelled into the living room.

Libby's father was asleep on the sofa. Libby had to yell because her older brother, Carl, was playing the piano. Carl was playing boogie-woogie. Loud.

"I said it's chow time," Libby yelled louder.

Mr. Johnson lifted the newspaper off his face. "Come on, maestro!" he called to Carl.

At the dinner table Grandma Gert had the pot of mashed potatoes.

"Pass the potatoes around, please, Gert," Mr. Johnson said.

Grandma Gert couldn't hear. She piled more potatoes on her plate.

"You know what?" Libby said. "Boris

followed Annie Bananie to school today. I wish I had a dog to follow me! Mrs. Liebling said the dog had the best manners in the class.'' Libby giggled. ''Why can't I have a dog?''

''Aggh. Dog.'' Suddenly Grandma Gert could hear.

''So her dog followed her to school one day.'' Mr. Johnson laughed.

''Just like Mary and her little lamb,'' Carl said.

''Lamb?'' Grandma Gert looked up. ''Oh, good. We're having lamb. Somebody pass me the platter, will you?''

''No, Mom,'' Mrs. Johnson said. ''We're having meat loaf. Not lamb.''

Mr. Johnson took a piece of meat loaf off the platter. ''Looks delicious,'' he said.

''Looks burned!'' Carl mumbled.

Libby giggled.

The telephone rang. Mrs. Johnson went to answer it.

"Oh, hello, Annie Bananie," Mrs. Johnson said. "How nice, dear . . . but Libby's already having a delicious dinner." Mrs. Johnson smiled at Libby. "Please tell your mother thank you, Annie Bananie. Libby's hoping she'll get lucky and have you here for Lucky Lunch Day." Then Mrs. Johnson hung up the phone.

"Annie Bananie was inviting you to dinner tonight with her, and her mom, and Boris. They're going to the Spaghetti Factory," Mrs. Johnson said.

"Cool," Carl said. "Her dog eats spaghetti?"

"Why did you have to tell Annie Bananie I wanted her for Lucky Lunch Day?" Libby asked.

"I'm sorry, Cookie Pie," Mrs. Johnson said. "Was it supposed to be a secret?"

"I guess not," Libby said. "Everybody wants Annie Bananie to come to their house. Besides, Boris couldn't come here anyway, because of Grandma Gert. He came once and it was a disaster!"

Grandma Gert hated dogs. But right now Grandma Gert couldn't hear a thing.

"Oh my gosh!" Mrs. Johnson said. "I just remembered. The baby has a doctor's appointment on Lucky Lunch Day. I'm sorry, Cookie, but I can make the lunches before I go and Grandma Gert can serve you."

"That's okay by me," Grandma Gert said. Her mouth was full of meat loaf.

Libby wanted to die. Now the last person she wanted at her house for Lucky Lunch Day was Annie Bananie. Then Libby thought of Annie Bananie at the Spaghetti Factory. Annie Bananie had invited her there. Being invited out for dinner was much more important than just being picked out of a hat for lunch, anyway. Libby felt happy inside. She hoped she would stay this lucky forever.

Chapter

4

"Ready, cowpokes?" Mrs. Liebling asked. She put the ten-gallon hat on top of her desk. "Time to pick names for Lucky Lunch Day. Annie Bananie, can you shake up the ten-gallon hat?"

Everyone's name was written on a small piece of paper. Mrs. Liebling put all the names inside the hat.

"Hurry," Michael said. "The bell's going to ring."

Annie shook the hat.

"Shake and bake." Sifredo laughed.

"My mom's baking special cookies for

whoever comes to my house." Cindy smiled at Annie Bananie.

"Meow." Bonnie purred at Annie. "Whoever gets me gets a special surprise. My mom's ordering pizza. No sausage."

Libby smiled at Bonnie. Bonnie could have Annie Bananie to lunch. Libby knew Bonnie would have a cow when she found out Annie had invited Libby for dinner.

Calvin raised his hand. Calvin's dad worked at home. "I'm warning you guys," Calvin said. "Whoever comes to my house gets spaghetti. That's the only thing my dad knows how to cook."

"Spaghetti!" Bonnie shouted. "That's what we had last night. Me and Annie Bananie and Annie's mom and Boris went to the Spaghetti Factory. But Boris stayed in the car." Bonnie laughed. "Right, Annie?"

"Meow." Annie giggled.

Everybody looked at Annie Bananie and Bonnie. Libby's heart started pounding.

"Okay," Mrs. Liebling said. "Who wants to pick the first names?"

"I do! I do!" Bonnie shot her arm up in the air.

"I now pronounce you man and wife," Eddie said without looking up from his dandruff collection.

Everybody laughed.

"Hisssss, Snowman," Bonnie said. "Whoever gets you for Lucky Lunch Day has bad luck for life!"

Mrs. Liebling put down the hat.

Everyone got quiet.

"I like it when my wild mustangs turn back into human beings," she said. Then she reached into the hat and picked the first names.

"Nina will go to Debbie's," Mrs. Liebling said.

"Neigh." Nina smiled.

Mrs. Liebling picked the next names.

"Michael will go with Calvin," she said.

"Annie Bananie will go to Libby's house. And Eddie," Mrs. Liebling said. She picked another piece of paper from the hat. "Your Lucky Lunch Day partner is Bonnie."

Annie and Libby walked home together from school. Bonnie and Debbie were right behind them.

"I'm glad I got you for Lucky Lunch," Annie whispered to Libby. "I wanted you to go to the Spaghetti Factory first. Then my mom made me ask Bonnie."

"It's no big deal," Libby said.

"That's for sure!" Annie whispered. "We can go there anytime. When my mom works we eat out almost every night."

"Neigh," Nina called. "Wait for me!"

"Neigh, Nina," Annie called back.

"Oink, Debbie," Bonnie said. "You get Horse-face for lunch."

Nina laughed and snorted. "You got lucky, Libby! You got Annie Bananie!"

"Too bad you're going to miss the pizza," Bonnie said to Annie Bananie. "Boris could have come, too."

"You're just mad because you got the Snowman for Lucky Lunch Day," Debbie said.

"I don't care." Bonnie sneered at Debbie. "I'm going to be sick that day, anyway."

Bonnie ran ahead into her house.

"Hi-yaa!" Annie said. "Let's all gallop to my house. Boris is waiting for me. We're coming, my darling Boris." Annie laughed.

"We're coming, my darling Boris." Debbie laughed.

"Neigh, Boris," Nina called.

"Hi-yaa! Giddyup!" Libby followed last in line.

When she got to her house, Libby trotted up the driveway. Everybody else could play. But Libby had work to do. She had to plan the best Lucky Lunch Day in history.

Chapter

5

For once the house was quiet.

"Hi, Libby," Grandma Gert whispered. "The baby is asleep."

"So what does that mean?" Libby asked. "I can't breathe?"

"Shhh!" Grandma Gert said loudly.

"Waaaaa." The baby woke up.

"Aggh." Grandma Gert threw her hands in the air. "I need this like a hole in the head."

The kitchen door slammed.

"I'm home!" Carl shouted. Then he started playing boogie-woogie.

Libby closed her bedroom door. She

took a piece of paper out of her notebook. Across the top of the paper she wrote:

THINGS LIBBY NEEDS FOR
LUCKY LUNCH DAY

1. New grandmother.

Libby left her room. Her mother was in the kitchen. She had her purse and keys out.

"Where are you going?" Libby asked.

"I have to run a few errands, Cookie Pie. Want to come with?"

"Yes!" Libby said. She ran ahead to the car.

"I got Annie Bananie for Lucky Lunch," Libby said to her mother.

Mrs. Johnson started the car. "Wow! You got lucky, Cookie Pie. I'll go straight to the vegetable section."

Libby panicked. "We're not going to the grocery store, are we?"

"Don't worry," Mrs. Johnson said. "I won't go grocery shopping until Sunday. You've got the whole weekend to decide what you want."

"Well, I can tell you already, no vegetables," Libby said. "Just because Annie Bananie's a vegetarian doesn't mean she wants vegetables."

"Oh," Mrs. Johnson said. "How about grilled cheese?"

"Boring," Libby said.

"Spaghetti's always good," Mrs. Johnson said.

"Annie Bananie can have real spaghetti at the Spaghetti Factory any night she wants," Libby said. "Besides, Calvin's already having spaghetti."

"Excuse me, Cookie," Mrs. Johnson said, "but I thought Lucky Lunch Day was about having a friend over. I didn't know it was a contest to see who can have the best lunch."

Libby looked at her mother. Her mother didn't understand a thing.

"The food's just part of what makes a good lunch," Mrs. Johnson said. "You and Annie will have a wonderful time. I'll get whatever you want. I'll cook it before I go. Then all Grandma Gert has to do is serve you."

"Like a waitress?" Libby asked.

"Aggh." Mrs. Johnson giggled. "Can I take your order?"

Libby laughed. She knew what she wanted for lunch was impossible. No matter what her mother made, the best Lucky Lunch Day in history could never be at Libby's house. Even if Grandma Gert wasn't there.

Mrs. Johnson turned into a parking lot. "First stop, jewelry store," she said.

"I'll wait here," Libby said. "I have to think about Lucky Lunch Day."

Then Libby thought as hard as she

could. No ideas were coming. Just then she saw something out of the corner of her eye. Two men were hanging a banner across the windows of a new store. The banner said:

GRAND OPENING—BUFFALO BILL'S

A third man came out of the store. He was carrying a cow under one arm and a horse under the other.

"We need a buffalo!" the first man shouted.

"Folks won't be able to get in the door with all them animals," the second man said. He sounded like a cowboy.

"Besides," the third man said, "that's too much meat!"

The three men laughed and patted each other on the back. Then they went inside.

Libby got out of the car to get a better look. The cow and horse were made out of plastic. The smell of onion rings and fresh paint was coming from inside. Buffalo Bill's wasn't a store. Buffalo Bill's was a restaurant. There was a big velvet picture of Buffalo Bill in the doorway. Cowboy music was playing and there were saddles hanging on the walls. They probably had milk shakes and french fries and vegetarian. The man had just said they didn't want too much meat.

Libby knew how she could have the best Lucky Lunch Day ever, after all. Annie Bananie wasn't coming to her house. Annie Bananie was going to Buffalo Bill's. Annie would tell everyone she and Libby were best friends. This was the best idea Libby ever had. Now all Libby had to do was figure out how to pay for the lunch.

Chapter

6

Saturday morning Libby stayed in her room. At the top of a clean piece of paper she wrote:

LIBBY'S PROBLEMS FOR LUCKY LUNCH DAY
  1. How to pay for lunch
    (a) My savings

Libby had $19.52 in her piggy bank. But she would have to smash the bank open, and somebody would hear her. Then she wrote:

(b) Earn money quick!
(c) How?

Libby stared at the paper. She stuck her finger into her mouth. She knew she had a wobbly tooth in there. If she could get that tooth loose enough she could yank it out tonight. Then she would tell the tooth fairy. By tomorrow morning there would be three dollars under Libby's pillow. But three dollars wouldn't be enough. Libby needed more teeth. At least four more if she was going to pay for lunch.

Libby didn't have any baby teeth left. The baby was the one with the baby teeth. Libby wrote:

(d) Steal baby's baby teeth.

Libby wadded up the paper fast. No one could ever see she wrote that. Besides, the baby didn't have any baby teeth yet, anyway! Libby took out another piece of paper. At the top of her new paper she wrote:

WHAT TO TELL MOMMY TO GET OUT OF HAVING LUCKY LUNCH DAY AT OUR HOUSE
(a) Ask if we can go to Buffalo Bill's.

Libby scratched that out. That was a ridiculous idea. Her mother would never say yes. Libby threw herself across her bed. She decided she wouldn't leave her room until she figured out every detail for Lucky Lunch Day.

Suddenly she heard a loud bark. She looked out the window. Boris was looking right up at her. But Annie Bananie was walking through Libby's back door. Libby hid her paper. She ran down the hall. Annie was already talking to Libby's mother and Grandma Gert in the kitchen.

"I can't wait to come for Lucky Lunch Day," Annie said.

"Us too," Mrs. Johnson said. "We're all looking forward to it."

Grandma Gert smiled. Then she looked out the window to make sure Boris wasn't trying to break into the house.

"And don't worry," Annie said to Grandma Gert. "I already told Boris he's not invited."

Libby came into the room. "Well, there's the little cookie," Mrs. Johnson said.

"Hello, Little Cookie," Annie Bananie said in her friendliest voice. "Want to come to my house before I have to go shopping with my mother?"

"Yeah," Libby said. "Let's get out of here before Boris dies of boredom." She giggled.

"See you on Lucky Lunch Day," Annie Bananie called.

The baby screamed. "I'll be lucky because the baby won't be here to scream through the whole lunch," Libby said. Then she pulled on Annie's sleeve.

"I wish I had a baby brother," Annie said as they ran out the door. "All Boris will ever be able to do is bark."

Libby ran around Annie Bananie's backyard. It was just Libby and Annie Bananie and Boris. Libby was Annie's second-best friend. For a moment Libby daydreamed that after Monday she could take Boris's place.

Annie's mother, Joy, came out and started the car. Libby watched Annie Bananie and Boris and Joy drive away. Libby felt good inside. She thought maybe she didn't have to take Annie Bananie to Buffalo Bill's after all. Lunch at her house could be good enough. She could tell her mom to get a frozen pizza. Grandma Gert could even dress up like a waitress. Libby started for home.

"Meooowww!" Bonnie sprang out from the bushes.

"Yeooww!" Libby jumped.

Bonnie fell on the lawn laughing. She scampered in the grass like a frisky little kitty.

"Want to play cat?" she asked.

"No thanks," Libby said. "And I don't think you're very funny."

"Meow. Get a life." Bonnie giggled. "I'll go ask Annie Bananie to play."

"Don't bother," Libby said. "She just left. I was just over there."

"Meow." Bonnie hissed. "You think you're the Queen of Switzerland because you got Annie Bananie for Lucky Lunch Day."

"No I don't," Libby said. "At least I'm not going to fake being sick that day. I feel sorry for Snowman. He won't have anywhere to go for lunch."

"I feel sorry for Annie Bananie." Bonnie giggled. "She's going to your house. No offense, but your mom's food is gross and your grandma cooks worse."

"It's not so disgusting," Libby said. "Besides, how do you know we're not going to have a surprise cook?"

"Like who?" Bonnie laughed. "I'm coming to school. I'll have the Snowman for lunch. It will be worth it just to see Annie Bananie's face after she's eaten at your house. I'll bet you she gets sick."

"Yeah, right," Libby said.

"Annie just better be out of the hospital by next Friday night," Bonnie said. "She's coming for a sleepover at my house."

"Said who?" Libby asked.

"Her mom said she could if she wants to," Bonnie said.

"Well, maybe she won't want to," Libby said. "I know Annie Bananie. I'm better friends with her than you are."

"If Annie Bananie gets sick on Lucky Lunch Day she'll be my best friend," Bonnie said. "If she doesn't she'll be yours. Okay? Bet?"

"Bet," Libby said.

Libby ran back to her house. She went straight to her room. She smashed open her bank and took out the $19.52. She didn't care if anybody heard her. Nothing could be more important than Lucky Lunch Day.

Libby took out her paper. She sat in bed. And she sat there writing until she figured out every last part of her plan.

Chapter

7

Monday morning Libby woke up early. She looked across the street to see if the lights were on in Annie's house. She listened to her father leaving for work. Then she went into her parents' room. Her mother was still asleep.

"Mommy," Libby said softly. "I have bad news about Annie Bananie."

"Tell Grandma Gert, Cookie," Mrs. Johnson mumbled. "She's going to get you off to school today. I was up all night with the baby."

Libby smiled at the baby in his crib. For the first time, she liked him. He was making this even easier than Libby had planned.

Libby put on her favorite dress. She took her savings and hid it in her backpack. Then she went into the kitchen. Grandma Gert was at the stove.

"I've got some bad news about Annie Bananie," Libby said.

"Aggh," Grandma Gert said. "It does look a little cloudy. Sit down and eat. I made potatoes."

"But I have to tell you something," Libby said louder. "Annie Bananie can't come here for Lucky Lunch Day. I just got a phone call."

"I didn't hear the phone ring," Grandma Gert said.

Libby's heart pounded fast. "That's because it only rang once," she said quickly. "Then I picked it up. Annie Bananie is sick. She's not even going to school today. So can I go to Bonnie's instead?"

"The one who thinks she's a cat?" Grandma Gert asked. "I suppose it's all right. I'll tell your mother. But I don't know what she'll do with the frozen pizza she bought for you and the Bananie girl."

"I'm sorry," Libby said.

"Aggh, don't worry," Grandma Gert said. "I'll eat it for my lunch. Maybe I'll cook it first."

After breakfast Libby ran to Annie Bananie's.

"You're early!" Annie laughed. "And we stayed up too late last night. See?"

Libby looked at Boris. He was fast asleep under the table.

"We have to go now!" Libby said. "I've got to tell you something really important."

"Okay." Annie laughed. She kissed Boris good-bye. She grabbed part of a muffin and stuffed it into her mouth. "But

I'm going to be starved by lunchtime. I can't wait!''

"Well, that's what I want to tell you about," Libby said. "Wait until you hear this—"

"Neigh!" Nina called. "You guys, wait for the Pony Express."

"Wait for the Piggy Express," called Debbie. She oinked and squealed as she ran along the sidewalk to catch up.

Libby started to walk faster. "Let's walk without them today," she said to Annie. "I've got to tell you the surprise!"

"Meoooow." Bonnie sprang out of her house.

"Purr," Annie called to Bonnie, "I thought you were going to be sick."

"I changed my mind," Bonnie said. "Didn't Libby tell you?"

"Hissss." Libby laughed.

"Is that the surprise, Libby?" Annie

giggled. Then, before Libby could answer, Annie started to gallop. "Come on, everybody," she said. "Follow me!"

Then everyone galloped behind her. All the way to school.

Chapter

8

"Okay, my cowpokes," Mrs. Liebling said at 11:45, "time for lunch. And remember, everybody has to be back in their saddles by exactly ten minutes to one. Have fun!"

"Yahoo!" Eddie yelled.

Bonnie pouted. "Me and Eddie will walk with you guys, Libby," she said. "Okay?"

"Sorry," Libby said. "We've got to take a special route."

"What's the special route?" Bonnie snapped. "Straight to the emergency room?"

"Come on, Cat Woman," Eddie called. "It's not polite to keep company waiting." Then he chased her. Bonnie ran across the playground screaming.

"Let's go, Libby." Annie laughed. "We've got to get to your house."

"No we don't," Libby said. "That's what I have to tell you. My mom forgot she had to take the baby to the doctor today. So she gave me money instead so we can go out to lunch. I bet you've never been where we're going before. It's the best place."

"Oh," Annie said. "But I wanted to go to your house. I like it there."

"Well, we have to go to the restaurant," Libby said. She talked fast because she was afraid she would start to cry.

"I better call my mom," Annie said.

"You don't have to," Libby said. "It's only two blocks away. It's like the Old West."

"Well, then, let's go, pardner," Annie said. Her voice was big and happy. "I'm hungry."

"I'm so hungry I could eat a buffalo." Libby laughed.

"Not me." Annie laughed. "I'm a vegetarian."

Libby and Annie Bananie ran all the way to Buffalo Bill's. Annie walked up to the plastic cow.

"Mooo!" She laughed. "I like this place. It's funny!"

"I told you," Libby said. She felt good inside.

A man dressed like a cowboy said, "Howdy, girls." He walked Annie and Libby to a table and put two menus down. "Any words you can't read, just let me know." He chuckled.

Libby and Annie Bananie opened their menus. Across the top of the menus it said:

BUFFALO BILL'S BURGERS
Hamburger
Cheeseburger
Double Hamburger
Double Cheeseburger
Ranch-Style Double Hamburger
  with Double Cheese

Libby's heart beat like a drum. There wasn't a single vegetable on the menu. The man came back over to the table.

"So what's it gonna be?" he asked.

"Is this an authentic Western restaurant?" Annie asked.

"You betcha," the man said.

"Don't you have grilled cheese sandwiches?" Annie asked.

"Nope," the man said.

"Do you have pizza?" Annie asked.

"Nope," the man said.

"Well, do you have anything besides hamburgers?" Libby asked.

"Of course we do," the man said. "We got baked beans and french fries."

"On my uncle's ranch you can get authentic Western omelettes," Annie said.

"We got milk shakes and onion rings," the man said. He tapped his pencil fast on the table.

"May I please have a cheeseburger and french fries?" Libby said quickly.

"Hey, Bill," the man shouted into the kitchen. *"Burn me a cow and then melt one. And a side of Pierres."*

Then he turned to Annie Bananie.

"Make mine baked beans and a vanilla shake," Annie said.

"That's it?" the man asked. "You'll still be hungry."

"Oh," Annie said. "Then I'll also have a large order of french fries and a chocolate milk shake. And maybe I'll have onion rings for dessert."

"Good choice," the man said. Then he called back to the kitchen:

"Hey, Bill, gimme beans, a large fried Pierre and two shook-up moos—one black and one white."

"In a jiffy," the cook called back.

Annie Bananie giggled. Then she and Libby couldn't stop giggling until the food came.

"Here you go, darlin's," the man said. *"Bon appétit."*

Annie's face lit up. "My mom would never let me eat this stuff for lunch." She laughed.

"Mine neither." Libby laughed too. She took the biggest bite of cheeseburger she could fit in her mouth.

Annie ate one french fry after another. Then she started on the dish of beans.

"Which milk shake are you going to drink first?" Libby asked.

Just then she saw the clock. It was twenty to one.

"Yikes!" she said. "We've gotta hurry."

"Okay," Annie said. She stuck one straw into the vanilla milk shake and one straw into the chocolate. Then she drank as fast as she could.

"Here you go, Buffalo Girls," the man said. He put the check on the table. "By the way, what are you two, sisters?"

"No." Annie laughed.

"We're best friends," Libby said. She couldn't believe she had said that. Annie sucked up the last ounce of chocolate milk shake.

"Come on, Buffalo Girl." Annie laughed. "We better gallop."

Chapter

9

"Well, here are my missing cow-girls," Mrs. Liebling said. Libby and Annie ran into the room. It was one o'clock.

Everybody was sitting on the carpet. That was where the class sat when they had something special to talk about.

"I'm sorry," Libby said. She was trying to catch her breath. Annie Bananie was sweating.

"I was just about to call your house," Mrs. Liebling said. "I was afraid you two were having so much fun that you wouldn't come back."

"We were having fun!" Libby said. "But we came back. See?"

Everyone looked at Libby and Annie Bananie.

"Meooowww, Annie Bananie," Bonnie said. "Sit next to me. There's room."

"Purr," Annie said softly. Then she sat down on the carpet right behind Libby. Libby felt good inside.

"You're just lucky Mrs. Liebling didn't call your house," Bonnie whispered to Libby.

Libby giggled. "How come?"

"I already called there," Bonnie whispered. "I was going to beg you to let me and the Snowman walk back with you guys. But your grandma said you weren't home. You were having Lucky Lunch at my house."

Then Bonnie smiled at Libby. "You're in trouble," she said.

"Excuse me, Bonnie," Mrs. Liebling said. "Is there something you want to tell all of us?"

Bonnie looked at Libby. "No, me-owww." She purred.

"Dandy," Mrs. Liebling said. "Then who wants to tell us about their Lucky Lunch Day?"

Sifredo raised his hand. "Me and Cindy had tacos," he said. "And her mom made flan for dessert."

"A flan is a Spanish pastry like a tart you fill with custard," Cindy said smartly. She smiled at Annie Bananie. "And it's vegetarian."

"*Sí.*" Sifredo winked. "It was pretty good, too."

"We had waffles," Nina called out.

"What, no hay?" Eddie laughed.

"We don't eat hay at my house." Debbie oinked.

"Well, you'd eat it if you ate at Bonnie's," Eddie said. "The pizza was like straw."

"You're just mad because it didn't have your favorite dandruff topping on it," Bonnie said.

"I put some on." Eddie smiled.

"Oh my gosh!" Bonnie screamed. "Vomit! Somebody get me a stomach pump."

"That's enough," Mrs. Liebling said. "Too many wild broncos in here. I sincerely hope your manners were better at lunch."

Everybody got quiet.

"I won the bet," Bonnie whispered to Libby.

"Did not," Libby said.

"You cheated," Bonnie whispered louder. "You had to have Annie at your house for lunch. Of course she wouldn't get sick if she ate someplace else!"

"Believe me," Libby whispered back

to Bonnie, "you're not Annie Bananie's best friend."

"Libby," Mrs. Liebling said. "Would you and Annie Bananie tell us about your Lucky Lunch?"

Everybody looked at Libby. Her heart pounded. "Ours was different than anybody's," Libby said. She tried not to sound like she was boasting. She turned around to Annie Bananie. "Should I tell them?" she asked.

"Uh-huh," Annie said. Then she looked down at the floor.

"We ate a Western-style lunch like on Annie Bananie's uncle's ranch. You would have loved it, Mrs. Liebling," Libby said. "And there was a horse there, and a cow."

"Your mom bought you a cow?" Michael asked.

"Cool," Calvin said.

"No." Libby laughed. "We ate at Buffalo Bill's. It's a brand-new restaurant for cowboys. They have a fake horse and a cow outside."

"Sounds like my kind of place," Mrs. Liebling said. "You sure are lucky, Annie Bananie."

"You know what, Mrs. Liebling?" Bonnie meowed. "Annie Bananie's coming to my house for a best friends' sleepover."

"Who said Annie Bananie's your best friend, Bonnie?" Libby said.

"Boris is Annie's best friend," Cindy said. "Right, Annie?"

"Uh-huh," Annie Bananie said. She put her hand on her forehead.

"I'd be your best friend if your mom took me to Buffalo Bill's," Sifredo said.

"That's what I'm trying to tell you," Bonnie said. "Libby's mother doesn't even know that—"

"So what kind of food did you have to eat, Libby?" Mrs. Liebling asked.

"I had a cheeseburger, and Annie Bananie had baked beans and two milk shakes and an order of fried Pierres." Libby giggled.

Debbie oinked. "What's a fried Pierre?"

Annie raised her hand.

"It's a secret code." Libby smiled. She could tell that everybody knew she and Annie were best friends. Even if Annie hadn't said the words yet.

Annie raised her hand higher.

"Annie Bananie is the only one who has the good manners to have her hand up," Mrs. Liebling said. "So, Annie, would you tell us something about Buffalo Bill's?"

Annie Bananie put her hand over her mouth. Her face turned white. Then, before anyone could move, Annie threw up. She threw up all over Libby's back.

Chapter

10

"Yeooww!" Bonnie sprang off the carpet. "Get her away from me!"

Annie Bananie raised her hand again.

"Heads up!" Eddie yelled.

Annie burped. Then she threw up again. This time longer.

Now the only two people left on the carpet were Annie Bananie and Libby. Annie rocked from side to side. Then she stood up slowly. Libby couldn't move. All she could feel was hot vomit drying on her back.

Mrs. Liebling put her arm around

Annie Bananie. "It's okay," Mrs. Liebling said. "You didn't do anything wrong."

"She splattered me!" Bonnie shouted. "I told her she'd get sick if she ate with Libby. Look! That's puke on my sweater!"

"It's milk shake." Debbie giggled.

"Stinky." Nina neighed.

"Gross!" Sifredo laughed.

"She can't help it!" Cindy said. "Annie Bananie's not disgusting on purpose."

"Yeah, you guys," Eddie said. Then he licked a stack of dandruff off his fingernail. "Get a life! How'd you like to be Libby right now?"

"I don't mind," Libby said. She turned slowly. Everybody got quiet.

Annie Bananie looked right at Libby. Annie put her hands over her face. Then, before she could stop herself, she burst into tears.

"Thank you, Libby!" Annie Bananie cried. "Only a best friend wouldn't be mad when somebody puked all over them."

"I know," Libby said. Then Libby couldn't stop crying, even though she felt happy inside.

Mrs. Liebling put two warm washcloths across Libby's and Annie Bananie's foreheads.

"You're two brave Buffalo Girls," Mrs. Liebling said. "The rest of the class go outside to the playground. I'll get the janitor to clean up here and I'll call your mothers."

"Man," Eddie said. "They both get to go home for the rest of the day?"

"But I should go with Annie Bananie and Libby," Bonnie said.

"Go rinse your sweater sleeve in the bathroom, Bonnie," Mrs. Liebling said.

"Then you can change into your gym clothes."

"Meowwww. But—"

"You'll be okay," Mrs. Liebling said to Bonnie. "I'll bet the ranch on it."

"You don't have to call my mother, Mrs. Liebling," Libby said. Her heart was beating like a drum. "It's not so bad."

"I'll be right back." Mrs. Liebling smiled at Libby. "Besides, your mom will want to know what happened since she just dropped you off from lunch."

Annie Bananie and Libby watched Mrs. Liebling close the door. They giggled. Then they burst into tears.

"At least your mom knows where you went for lunch!" Annie cried.

"I'm sorry," Libby said. "My mom's going to kill me, too. She didn't really give me that money for Buffalo Bill's." Libby sobbed. "She doesn't even know I

went there. I just wanted your Lucky
Lunch Day to be special.''

''It was!'' Annie cried. Then she closed
her eyes and fell asleep.

Mrs. Liebling came back into the
room.

''I called your house, Libby,'' she said.
''Your mother wasn't even home. But
your grandmother told me that after your
mom dropped you girls off, she had to run
an errand.''

''Uh-huh,'' Libby said.

''So your grandma's on her way,'' Mrs.
Liebling said. ''She's coming to get you.
And Annie Bananie is going to your house
until her mom picks her up. Her mom
just left her office. Don't worry. Everything's going to be fine.''

''Uh-huh,'' Libby said. She could
hardly breathe. She looked over at Annie
Bananie. Annie was in a chair, snoring.

When Grandma Gert came, Mrs.

Liebling walked Libby and Annie Bananie and Grandma Gert to the car. Libby was just glad they didn't have to walk across the playground.

Libby sat next to Grandma Gert. Annie Bananie climbed into the backseat. Then she fell asleep again. Grandma Gert didn't say a thing.

"That was nice of you to not tell Mrs. Liebling the truth," Libby said.

"I'll leave that to you," Grandma Gert said. "I don't even know what the truth is. Do you?"

"Yes," Libby said.

"That's a good start," Grandma Gert said. "You can tell your mother the whole thing. She should be back with the baby by now."

Grandma Gert drove about six miles an hour. A big truck behind her honked. Grandma Gert didn't hear the truck horn, but she did hear Libby softly crying.

"Besides the vomit, how was your lunch?" Grandma Gert asked.

"Pretty good," Libby said. "How was the pizza?"

"How do I know?" Grandma Gert asked. "I had potatoes. I figured I'd save the pizza for the next time Annie Bananie comes for lunch."

"Thank you, Grandma," Libby said.

"Aggh," Grandma Gert said. "Aggh."

Here is a sample chapter from

Read what happens when
Annie Bananie first moves to town
and meets Libby Johnson
and her friends!

Chapter 2

"I'm Annie Bananie," the girl said. She had a big, friendly voice. "Do you want to play with me?"

"Okay," Libby said. She looked at Boris. She was trying not to act too excited.

"Oh, goody!" Annie said. She was very excited. "What's your name?"

"Libby Johnson," Libby said. "It doesn't rhyme or anything. I like your dog. Can I pet him?"

"Of course," Annie Bananie said. "He's superfriendly. Boris, this is our new friend, Libby. Give Libby paw."

Boris shook hands. Then he drooled on Libby's foot.

"Is this your house?" Annie asked. "Can we come in to play?"

Libby looked to make sure Grandma Gert wasn't looking out the window.

"It's just an ordinary house," Libby said. "Want to see something more fun?"

"Sure," Annie said. "Follow me!" Annie acted like she had lived on Barry Avenue for years.

"I'm going to Nichols School," Annie said.

"That's where I go," Libby said.

"I'm going to be in Mrs. Liebling's class," Annie said.

"She's my teacher, too," Libby said, smiling.

"Oh, wow!" Annie said. "I'm so lucky! Do you have a dog that Boris can play with?"

"No," Libby said. "But I'm probably going to get one."

"Oh, goody!" Annie laughed. "Then we'll have everything the same."

"Except you've got the best name," Libby said. "Is it real?"

"No," Annie said. "I made it up. My name was Ann. But that's so boring. Come on. Let's run!"

For the first time all day, Libby felt happy. She ran after Annie Bananie and Boris all the way to their new house.

"Mommy!" Annie Bananie called. "Quick, hurry! I have a new friend!"

Libby liked Annie's mother. Her name was Joy.

"I'm so happy to meet you," Joy said to Libby.

Then she shook Libby's hand like Libby was a businesswoman. Libby liked that.

"Come on in, Libby," Joy said. "Just step over the boxes."

Libby followed Annie Bananie. Annie had the best room. The phone man was putting in Annie's own phone line. The moving man brought in Annie's computer and two crates

of tapes. Annie had about a thousand dress-
es and hats. She also had two rats named
Walnut and Peanut, a hamster, and an old
cat. And best of all, Libby thought, Annie
had Boris and no brothers. No piano. No
grandmother. Nobody making a lot of
noise. Annie's father wasn't there. Libby figured he was at work.

"Let's go," Annie said to Libby. Boris's ears
perked up.

"We're leaving," Annie sang out to her
mother.

"Put on something clean and pretty," Joy
called out from the living room. "And don't
go too far."

"Oh, brother!" Annie rolled her eyes.
Then she pulled a perfect white T-shirt out
of her closet and changed as fast as she
could.

"Follow me!" she said.

Libby couldn't figure out where Annie
was going.

"Aye, Matey Boris," Annie called out. "Grab a fishing pole."

Boris picked up a stick off the ground and followed Annie. She was headed straight for the alley.

Libby never went into the alley except when she was throwing out the garbage. Now Libby couldn't believe it. There was Annie Bananie hanging halfway inside a garbage can.

"Aye, Matey Libby," Annie called. "Hand me Boris's pole, please."

At first Annie used the fishing pole to dig deeper and deeper into the garbage can. Then she called out, "Boris! Prepare the deck!"

Annie slowly lifted something up on the pole like she was reeling it in. At the end of the pole, Libby saw somebody's old necklace. It was filthy and made out of blue plastic that was supposed to look sparkly.

"Oh my gosh!" Annie said. Her face lit up. She spread the necklace out on the palms of her hands so that Libby and Boris could see.

"Look, Mateys!" Annie said. "Diamonds!"

She poured the necklace slowly into Libby's hands.

"Aye, Matey," Annie said. "This is for you. My first new friend. Treasure it always."